Pub.
4.08
W9-ASC-234
FEB 1986
RECEIVED
OHIO DOMINICAN
COLLEGE LIBRARY
COLUMBUS, OHIO
43219

MITZI and the Terrible Tyrannosaurus Rex

OTHER YEARLING BOOKS YOU WILL ENJOY:

TALES OF A FOURTH GRADE NOTHING, *Judy Blume*

SUPERFUDGE, *Judy Blume*

OTHERWISE KNOWN AS SHEILA THE GREAT, *Judy Blume*

ARE YOU THERE GOD? IT'S ME, MARGARET., *Judy Blume*

BLUBBER, *Judy Blume*

IGGIE'S HOUSE, *Judy Blume*

BEEZUS AND RAMONA, *Beverly Cleary*

ELLEN TEBBITS, *Beverly Cleary*

RAMONA THE PEST, *Beverly Cleary*

RAMONA QUIMBY, AGE 8, *Beverly Cleary*

YEARLING BOOKS are designed especially to entertain and enlighten young people. Charles F. Reasoner, Professor Emeritus of Children's Literature and Reading, New York University, is consultant to this series.

For a complete listing of all Yearling titles, write to Dell Publishing Co., Inc., Promotion Department, P.O. Box 3000, Pine Brook, N.J. 07058.

MITZI and the Terrible Tyrannosaurus Rex

by Barbara Williams

illustrated by
Emily Arnold McCully

A YEARLING BOOK

Published by
Dell Publishing Co., Inc.
1 Dag Hammarskjold Plaza
New York, New York 10017

ISBN: 0-440-45673-8

Reprinted by arrangement with E. P. Dutton, Inc.
Printed in the United States of America
First Yearling printing—August 1983
CW

for three special people—
Peter Siddoway, who taught himself
to read when he was two;
Gil Williams, who taught himself
to read when he was in college; and
Karen Williams, who is teaching herself
to live with a terrible and wonderful
Tyrannosaurus Rex

Contents

1

The Book and the Boots

Mitzi McAllister's stomach felt like a balloon sailing up to the clouds. She could hardly wait to show her mother the book her teacher had given her.

Clutching it, Mitzi rushed to the cloakroom, where her green parka was the only coat still hanging on a hook. As she grabbed it she squinted at her boots, on the cloakroom floor, and at the brown paper bag beside them.

Mitzi's mother taught at the university and sometimes acted like a schoolteacher. She had insisted Mitzi wear those ugly old things today, just because there was some fresh snow on the ground.

But Mitzi wanted to wear her brand-new yellow canvas shoes with blue stripes. She had argued that the sun would melt the snow soon. Finally they agreed that Mitzi could carry the new shoes in a paper bag, but she had to walk to and from school in those yucky old boots.

Mitzi scowled at the boots on the cloakroom floor. It would delay her to change back into them. And she was impatient to show her mother this wonderful schoolbook and to deliver the exciting message from Mrs. Fotheringham.

On Monday Mitzi would be promoted to the Red reading group, the group of top readers who got special privileges. Soon Mitzi would be among them, feeding goldfish and watering plants while the Yellows and Blues stammered and guessed their way through easy books. At last Mitzi had proof for her mother that she was "living up to her potential."

"It's too hot outside to wear boots," Mitzi told herself so loudly that Mr. Ledgard overheard.

"Yep," agreed the janitor. "It's right nice outside now. March snowstorms never last long."

Encouraged by this unexpected support from an adult, Mitzi made a decision. "I think I'll carry my boots home in this paper bag."

"Good idea," said Mr. Ledgard, looking at her with shiny blue eyes. He was a small man in overalls that seemed big. "I'll help you."

Mitzi watched the gentle way he set his broom against the wall. She wondered if he were mar-

ried. Maybe her mother would like to marry Mr. Ledgard instead of Walter.

"Won't fit," Mr. Ledgard announced as the bag began to rip. "Guess we'll have to tuck them under your arm. How's that?"

"Fine," said Mitzi. "Thanks."

"What's that book you've got there?" he asked.

"Oh, that's the book the Red reading group just finished. I have to bring a note from my mother saying I read it aloud to her. I'm going to be promoted to the Red group on Monday if I can read this book over the weekend."

"Of course you can read it," said Mr. Ledgard with a friendly pat on her shoulder. "Anyone as spunky as you should be a Red. You're about the spunkiest girl in this whole school."

Really? thought Mitzi, giddy from so much praise. If her mother wanted to get married to someone, why couldn't it be to an understanding man like Mr. Ledgard?

As they walked to the outside door together, Mitzi imagined a perfect family scene. Her mother and Mr. Ledgard sat cozily on the sofa while Mitzi read aloud to them from one of the Red group's hard books.

Mr. Ledgard held the door open for her. "I know you can do it," he said.

Waving happily, Mitzi exploded out the door of Amelia Earhart Elementary School. She darted across the playground and began chugging up the sidewalk on Roosevelt Avenue.

"HOLD IT!" cried the crossing guard, sticking her pole across Mitzi's path. Crossing guards were bossy sixth graders who made everyone stop at the corner, for no reason at all.

On another day, Mitzi might have frowned at the tall girl in the orange cap. But right now she felt too happy to frown at anyone.

Besides, she was secretly grateful for a chance to catch her breath. She studied the title of the book. *"Let's Go to an In—"* she read silently. *"Let's Go to an In—In—In—"*

"Okay," said the crossing guard, removing the pole. "You can go now."

Mitzi remembered to walk briskly across the street. Crossing guards yelled at people who either dawdled or ran. But she resumed speed on the other side, trotting up Roosevelt Avenue until she came to University Street.

Once more she stopped to catch her breath. This time she looked at the illustration on the cover for a clue to the name of the book. The drawing showed a building of some sort. It wasn't like any building Mitzi had ever seen, but it looked like fun—a great place to play hide-and-seek. Or hold a club meeting.

Mitzi struggled again to read the title of the book. *"Let's Go to an In—In—Indian—"* That was it. *Indian,* she decided triumphantly. *"Let's Go to an Indian Clubhouse."*

"RARF, RARF," said Rosie, the big Doberman pinscher who lived in the house on University Street that had the interesting orchard. A sign on the fence said BEWARE OF DOG, but Mitzi wasn't fooled. She knew the owners wanted people to think Rosie was a mean dog, so they wouldn't sneak into the orchard in the summer to steal the fruit.

"Hi, Rosie, old girl," said Mitzi. "Are you lonely?"

"RARF," said Rosie.

Mitzi set the bundles from both her arms on the sidewalk and opened the gate just wide enough to thrust one hand through the crack. "Good girl," she told the dog as she petted Rosie behind the ears and under the chin.

"You better watch out," called a woman from the porch. "That dog is vicious. Shut that gate before she bites you."

"She won't bite me," said Mitzi. "Rosie's a nice dog. She likes me."

Rosie stuck her long snout through the crack in the gate and pushed it open wider.

Sniff, sniff, sniff, went Rosie at Mitzi's boots on the sidewalk.

"You go home before that dog bites you," the woman yelled.

Rosie stopped sniffing the boots and seized one of them in her teeth.

"You give that back!" demanded Mitzi, swinging the gate wide and charging after the dog.

"Get out of my yard!" called the woman.

"YOUR DOG STOLE MY BOOT!" wailed Mitzi angrily, partly because Rosie had already disappeared, and partly because Mitzi's new canvas shoes were covered with mud. "AND SHE MADE ME RUIN MY NEW SHOES!"

"Serves you right. Get out of my yard," said the woman.

Mitzi was torn. Should she try to find Rosie and the boot? Or should she protect her new shoes from more mud? The woman's angry face helped her decide. Mitzi scooted back out the gate, picked up her book and other boot from the sidewalk, and raced toward home.

Once there, Mitzi sneaked in the back way through the utility room, hiding her muddy shoes and the one boot behind the washing machine. Maybe she could slip the shoes into the washing machine when her mother wasn't home. And maybe she could go back later to find the boot Rosie had stolen.

"Is that you, Mitzi?" called her mother.

"Uh-huh," said Mitzi, arriving in the dining room, where her mother was setting the table with the best china.

"Where have you been?" said Dr. McAllister in her schoolteacher voice. "I told you to come straight home so you could get ready for the party." Luckily for Mitzi, she seemed too busy to notice her daughter's stocking feet.

"Oh," said Mitzi. "I forgot." She didn't see why her mother called it a party anyway. Walter was just coming to dinner with his mother and children so they could all meet each other. "I had to stay after school," said Mitzi.

"Oh Mitzi," wailed her mother.

"I didn't do anything bad," Mitzi explained quickly. "I did something good."

"Oh?" said her mother. "What did you do?"

"I lived up to my potential," said Mitzi.

Her mother's faint smile troubled Mitzi. "I thought you would be proud of me," Mitzi said.

Her mother set down the stack of dishes she was holding and gave Mitzi a hug. "Of course I'm proud of you. Tell me all about it."

"Mrs. Fotheringham is going to promote me to the Red reading group. But you have to hear me read this book first."

"Darling! That's wonderful! You can read it to me first thing tomorrow." Her mother picked up the dishes and continued setting the table.

"I can do it now," Mitzi offered, "while you set the table." She cleared her throat. *"Let's Go to an Indian Clubhouse,"* she began.

LET'S GO
TO AN
INDIAN
CLIFF
DWELLING

"An Indian *what*?" asked her mother.

"An Indian Clubhouse," said Mitzi.

"Let me see that," said her mother, looking over Mitzi's shoulder. "That says *Indian Cliff Dwelling,"* she explained. "That's a picture of Mesa Verde."

Mitzi hadn't minded too much being interrupted when she was only a Yellow. But if she were to live up to her potential in the Red group, she didn't think she should be corrected. "How do you know?" she challenged.

"Darling, I teach about Mesa Verde at the university."

Mitzi wasn't convinced. Teaching at the university had nothing to do with books the Reds used in third grade. "What's Mesa Verde?" she demanded.

"Mesa Verde is a cliff dwelling which Indians made in southwestern Colorado many hundreds of years ago."

"Are you sure?" Mitzi asked.

"Of course I'm sure," said her mother. "I'm an archaeologist. Archaeologists learn about people who lived and died a long time ago. My specialty is the ancient Indians of the Southwest. That includes Mesa Verde."

"What's a specialty?" asked Mitzi.

"A specialty is something you're good at because you've worked hard to master it," said her mother. "My specialty is also what I teach."

Mitzi felt uneasy. "How come your specialty is dead people?"

"That's what archaeology is all about. People who are dead. Haven't I ever explained that to you?"

"No," said Mitzi, disappointed. She had always known her mother was interested in Indians, but she didn't know her mother wasted the time of grown-up college students by teaching them about dead Indians. She wished her mother taught something important at the university, like typewriting, or how to drive a car.

"Mrs. Fotheringham probably wanted me to hear you read the book because she knew I could explain it to you," said her mother.

With a shrug, Mitzi opened the cover of the book to the first page of the story and began reading: " 'How would you like to live in a home . . .' "

Mitzi's mother banged the cabinet door open and pulled out the silver chest.

"You're not listening," said Mitzi.

"Darling, I'm sorry," said her mother. "This isn't a good time for us to read together. I'm very nervous right now. I'll read with you first thing tomorrow. I promise."

"All right," said Mitzi with a sigh. One of the

most important days of her life wasn't turning out very well.

"Now go take a bath and get dressed," said her mother. "I need you to help me."

"What are we having?" asked Mitzi.

"Fried chicken," said her mother.

"Do you want me to go to the Kentucky takeout for you?" Mitzi asked.

"Brace yourself for a shock, pal. I'm cooking the chicken myself. From scratch, if you'll pardon the expression." Her mother must have told a joke because she smiled. If so, Mitzi didn't get it. But at least she understood why her mother was nervous. Dr. McAllister didn't do a whole lot of scratch cooking.

"Now go take a bath and get dressed," said her mother. "I washed your blue slacks and laid them out for you. I thought they'd look nice with your new yellow and blue shoes."

"Oh," said Mitzi, remembering something terrible. She curled up her toes inside her wet blue socks. With her yellow and blue shoes covered with mud, what could she wear on her feet when Walter and his family arrived?

2

Walter's Family

"Mitzi, check to see if I put salt and pepper on the table. And a butter knife. And put two cubes of ice in each glass. Use the tongs, not your fingers."

Cooking chicken from scratch had somehow made her mother give orders faster and more shrilly. She had sent Mitzi back and forth from the kitchen to the dining room a million times, frequently to do the same job over again.

"And go take off those old shoes," said Mitzi's mother. "Walter and his family will be here any minute."

Any minute was right. The door opened and Walter's family walked in, without even knocking.

"Hello, everybody, we're here," called Walter.

"Hi," answered Mitzi's mother. "I'm in the kitchen. I can't leave this gravy."

"Mother, this is Mitzi," Walter said to an old

lady, and then he sailed right past Mitzi to get to the kitchen. Why didn't Walter ever talk to her? What would it be like to spend the rest of her life with a father who never talked to her?

Walter's mother did not follow Walter to the kitchen right away. She peered at Mitzi through thick glasses and then stooped down to talk to her. Mitzi could see her dangly purple earrings and where her gold hair was brown at the roots. "My, my, you're a tall girl, aren't you?"

It was one of those dumb grown-up questions that Mitzi never knew how to answer. She decided that Walter's mother probably meant it as a compliment and that she should say something nice in reply.

"Yes," said Mitzi. "You're tall, too, aren't you?"

Walter's mother stood up stiffly, as if she hadn't liked her compliment. Turning abruptly, she marched toward the kitchen. Maybe she was going to complain about Mitzi's manners.

Mitzi listened through the doorway, just in case. But all Walter's mother said was, "Can I help you, Patricia?"

"No thanks, Mother Potts," said Mitzi's mother. "It's your turn to be my guest. Sit down and talk to me while I stir this gravy."

Everyone seemed to know everyone else, except Mitzi. She felt lonely and awkward, a stranger in her own home. The worst thing of all was that through the doorway she could see Walter kissing her mother's neck. Mr. Ledgard would never kiss her mother's neck. At least not in public.

Walter's sons had lagged behind, walking slowly to study everything they passed. The smaller boy gazed at a cobweb, a tear in the wallpaper, and Mitzi herself, as if they were equally weird. The older boy finally spoke.

"I'm Frederick," he said. "Don't call me Fred or Freddy. My father hates nicknames." Frederick wore thick glasses like his father's and grandmother's and had freshly combed hair with a crooked part. He reminded Mitzi of all the school crossing guards she had ever met.

"I'm eleven," he continued. He wasn't very big for an eleven-year-old, and Mitzi was strong for eight. Those things would come in handy if he ever got too bossy with her.

He waved vaguely in the direction of the kitchen. "We call our grandmother Nana. That's the only nickname my father allows. You can call her Nana Potts."

Frederick pointed to his little brother with an elbow. "He's three. His name is Charles Darwin Potts, but we call him Darwin. Darwin isn't a nickname. It's a middle name, so it's allowed, but he won't answer if you call him that. He only answers when you call him Tyrannosaurus Rex." Frederick rolled his eyes at the ceiling. "He thinks he's a dinosaur."

"Grunch," said Charles Darwin Potts, also known as Tyrannosaurus Rex.

"Why is he wearing those?" said Mitzi, noticing the blue swim fins on Darwin's feet. "Is he going swimming?"

"Darwin can't swim, but it doesn't matter because he's a tyrannosaurus rex," said Frederick. "Those aren't swim fins. They're tyrannosaurus rex feet. Darwin falls down a lot, but dinosaurs lived dangerously. You have to take your chances if you're going to be one."

Mitzi wasn't sure she understood all of that. Frederick's conversation was making her dizzy.

"Grunch," said the dinosaur with tyrannosaurus rex feet. He had to remove the index finger of his left hand from his mouth before he could speak. It was a different color from all his other fingers. Dark pink.

"Grunch yourself," said Mitzi.

Darwin grinned up at her. "Grunch, grunch, grunch," he said, curling up both hands like claws. Then he put his left index finger back in his mouth and sucked at it furiously to make up for lost time.

A new emotion filled Mitzi. She stopped feeling sorry for herself and started feeling sorry for Darwin, who sucked his finger until it was raw and could only say "grunch." Her best friend, Elsie Wolf, had a little three-year-old sister who could talk lots better than Darwin.

Maybe Darwin had never learned to talk because Frederick never gave him a chance. Maybe Darwin never learned to talk because Walter didn't like his own son any better than he liked Mitzi, and he never talked to Darwin either. It must be very lonely to be three years old and not have a mother.

Suddenly Mitzi had a wonderful idea that might help Darwin and would probably solve one of her problems too. "I'll be right back," she told him and shot up the stairs to her bedroom. When she returned, she clunked down the steps slowly. Instead of messy old shoes, she was wearing stiff green ski boots.

"Hi, Tyrannosaurus Rex," she said to Darwin. "I'm a brontosaurus. See my brontosaurus feet? Say *bron-to-sau-rus.*"

"GRUNCH!" said Darwin, making claws with both hands and lunging after her.

Mitzi ducked. "I won't let you catch me until you say my name," she told him. "Say *bron-to-sau-rus.*"

"GRUNCH!" yelled the terrible Tyrannosaurus Rex.

Mitzi *clomp-clomp*ed around the dining-room table, through the hall, and into the living room, with Tyrannosaurus Rex *smack-smack*ing behind. *Clomp-clomp, smack-smack. Clomp-clomp, smack-smack.* "Grunch, grunch, grunch!"

When they reached the hall a second time, Darwin's swim fin caught against the coat rack. Dinosaur and rack fell to the ground with a clatter.

Mitzi's mother appeared instantly in the kitchen doorway. "Mitzi, what on earth is that racket?"

"Nothing," replied Mitzi. "Darwin and I were just playing dinosaur."

"Oh," said her mother lamely. "Well, try not to destroy the whole swamp."

Mitzi was tired of the game anyhow. She helped first Darwin and then the coat rack back into their upright positions.

BONNNG! came a noise from the dining room, where Frederick was holding the dinner gong. Mitzi had thought many times how much fun it would be to play orchestra with that beautiful brass gong, but her mother never let her touch it. Mitzi wondered if she should tell her mother what Frederick was doing.

Her mother seemed to know already. She took the gong from Frederick with a smile and set it back on the shelf. Then she called, "Come to dinner, Mitzi. You show Frederick and Darwin where their places are and help Darwin with his bib."

"GRRRRRRRRUNCH!" said Darwin, in a voice which obviously meant that dinosaurs didn't wear bibs. Despite his limited vocabulary, Mitzi was beginning to understand Darwin much better than she did Frederick. She certainly liked him better.

Mitzi boosted Darwin atop the big dictionary her mother had placed on a dining-room chair. "Look at the pretty bib," she said. "My mother bought it just for you. Look, it has Winnie-the-Pooh on it. Don't you want me to help you put it on?"

"Grunch," said Darwin, shaking his head vigorously.

"Darwin passed through the Pooh phase in January," Frederick reported. "Santa brought him the Pooh books for Christmas, so Darwin carried a pot of honey everywhere he went, even though he doesn't like honey and wouldn't eat it. I found my goldfish drowned in a sea of honey, and Nana was pasted to her sheets one night when she climbed into bed. Pooh was a less violent phase than Tyrannosaurus Rex, but it was messier. There are tradeoffs in everything, I guess." Frederick shook his napkin and set it on his lap.

How did Darwin paste his grandma to the

sheets? Mitzi wondered, as Walter came bustling into the room. He was carrying a huge tray, his sleeves rolled up to show thick arms covered with black hair. Mitzi watched his strong, square fingers setting bowls of gravy, mashed potatoes, chicken, and buttered carrots on the table.

Even Nana Potts was helping. She pushed aside the salt and pepper Mitzi had carefully arranged on the table to make room for a platter of red Jell-O salad. Mitzi shot the salad a worried look. Her mother was no Jell-O salad expert. This one oozed over the lettuce like wet poster paint.

Mitzi felt hurt at not being asked to help too. She decided to be useful in another way. "Can I put some salad on your plate?" she asked Darwin, scooping a big helping for him.

Darwin was no dummy. "Grunch!" he said with disgust.

Instead, he reached for the chicken. Mitzi didn't see the dinosaur claws coming, and red droplets of salad sprayed the air and fell to the ground like fireworks on the Fourth of July.

Mitzi eyed the red yuck on the carpet, wishing her mother had stuck to sliced tomatoes or canned peaches.

"Look what Darwin did," Frederick said righteously. He turned to his brother. *"You did that on purpose!"*

Darwin began to cry.

"Tell Patricia you're sorry, darling," Nana Potts said sweetly.

"It's nothing," said Mitzi's mother. "Mitzi can clean it up."

"Frederick can clean it up," Walter ordered.

Mitzi looked hopelessly at the gelatin splatters. Frederick looked angrily at Darwin. Then Frederick grabbed a plate and spoon and Mitzi rushed into the kitchen for a wet towel. Together they spooned and scrubbed, spooned and scrubbed. When they finished, the carpet still looked blotchy, but the grown-ups were too busy to notice. They had started eating. Very rude of them, Mitzi thought.

The grown-ups were talking to each other, too. Mitzi kept waiting for them to include her in their conversation, but they were discussing boring things like politics and how to raise more money for the university.

"You don't need to worry that my father's not a good carpenter," Frederick was saying.

"Mmm," commented Mitzi through her mouthful of mashed potatoes. She hadn't known that scratch potatoes were lumpier than Colonel Sanders' and therefore were harder to swallow.

"Just because he's a biology professor who writes important textbooks doesn't mean that he can't do practical things too," Frederick said.

"He'll do all the work himself, except for the wiring and plumbing, of course."

"What plumbing?" asked Mitzi.

"In the bathroom," said Frederick.

"Is your toilet broken?" asked Mitzi. Mitzi knew a lot about plumbers and broken toilets. She had once tried to flush away some bad spelling papers.

"It won't be my bathroom. It's Nana's. She can climb stairs perfectly well, so she doesn't need a bathroom on the first floor. But my father says you should always plan ahead. You never know how long your health will hold out and when you'll need a bedroom on the first floor."

Mitzi was confused. "I thought you were talking about a bathroom," she said.

"Yes, he's going to build her both a bedroom and a bathroom," Frederick said. "Nana's bedroom will be where your porch is, and her bathroom will be where the utility room is."

Suddenly understanding, Mitzi was worried. Frederick was talking as if the wedding between her mother and Walter were all settled. He was talking as if that lady with the gold and brown hair could put her bed on Mitzi's back porch without even asking.

Could Mitzi keep the marriage from happening by scaring Nana Potts away from her porch? She tried to remember all the things that Elsie Wolf's grandmother was afraid of. Maybe Mitzi could borrow some snakes from the zoo and hide them on her porch. Maybe she could find some mice. She wondered if Nana Potts were afraid of potato bugs.

"Your utility room will make a great bathroom," Frederick was saying.

"How do you know?" Mitzi argued. "You've never seen it."

"Yes, I have," he said.

"When?" she demanded.

"When you were upstairs putting on those brontosaurus feet." Frederick leaned close to whisper. "And I know why you put them on. I found your muddy shoes behind the washing machine."

"Oooh," Mitzi gasped.

"Don't worry. I won't tell," promised Frederick. "Listen, you and I have got to stick together. It's our only chance. We can't afford any sibling rivalry between you and me."

Mitzi didn't know what *sibling rivalry* meant, so she didn't know what Frederick was talking about. Also, she didn't care. All she cared about was that Frederick Potts was a nosy, bossy boy who talked too much. She didn't want him for a brother any more than she wanted Walter Potts for a father.

Was her mother really planning to marry Walter? How soon?

She had been so busy thinking about her problems that Mitzi hadn't noticed the phone was ringing. "I'll get it," she said at last, pleased at the chance to show Walter's family her nice telephone manners. Maybe Frederick had been allowed to ring the dinner gong, but Mitzi was sure he couldn't answer a telephone as politely as she could.

Before Mitzi could stand up, however, Darwin had already slid off his dictionary. He was *smack-smack*ing into the kitchen on blue tyrannosaurus rex feet.

Mitzi walked after him, a whirlpool of emotions spinning inside. Anger at Frederick. Resentment toward Walter and his mother. Disappointment at her own mother. Pity for poor Darwin, who had never learned to talk because he was caught in such a terrible family.

Well, Mitzi would let him say "grunch" into her telephone if it would make him happy. She kept herself from interfering while he picked up the receiver.

"Hello," said Tyrannosaurus Rex in perfect English, not even tripping over his *L*'s as Elsie Wolf's little sister would have done. Mitzi's mouth fell open. "I'm sorry," Darwin continued, as politely as Mitzi would have spoken herself. "Mitzi can't come to the phone. Can I take a message? Okay. Good-bye."

Mitzi stared in disbelief as Darwin hung up the receiver and walked to his grandmother. "Nana, what's a message?"

All the grown-ups cracked up. Frederick and Mitzi scowled.

"Isn't he adorable?" cooed Nana Potts. "You just never know what's going to come out of him next."

"What's a message?" Darwin repeated.

Mitzi's mother put on her schoolteacher expression. "When you ask someone if you can take a message, you are asking the person if you can tell something to someone else. Did the person on the phone have something to say that you should tell Mitzi?"

"No," said Darwin.

"Who was it?" asked Mitzi.

Darwin shrugged.

"Why didn't you call me to the phone?" Mitzi could hear herself screaming.

"You aren't supposed to bother people when they're eating," Darwin explained.

The grown-ups laughed again, even louder.

"Isn't he adorable?" Nana Potts repeated.

"I wasn't eating!" screamed Mitzi. *"I was standing right next to you!"*

"Please stop yelling, Mitzi," said her mother. She turned to Darwin. "Can't you tell Mitzi who telephoned her?"

"Grunch," said the dinosaur. He paddled his rubbery blue feet toward the television set in the living room, and suddenly the house was filled with loud voices and tinny laughter.

"Sit down please, Mitzi, and finish your dinner," said her mother. "If the call was important, the person will phone back again."

Mitzi couldn't believe what was happening. Wasn't anyone going to scold Darwin? Wasn't anyone going to tell him to turn off the television set? Wasn't anyone going to make *him* sit down and finish *his* dinner?

Frederick punched Mitzi gently and whispered in her ear. "Sometimes Darwin is almost as adorable as a rattlesnake. Can you understand why you and I have to stick together?"

3

The Genius

Being a good hostess meant smiling and pretending that life was fair, even though it wasn't. Right after the apple pie and coffee, her mother had taken Mitzi into the bathroom for a lesson in good hostessing.

Good hostesses, for instance, did not scream at little guests who failed to call them to the telephone. Good hostesses did not tattle about how many drumsticks their guests had wasted. Good hostesses did not sulk when they were asked to take young company upstairs, instead of going into the living room where they could listen to the things the grown-ups were discussing.

Mitzi had several reasons for wanting to stay in the room where the grown-ups were talking. For one reason, she had an uneasy feeling that wedding plans might be decided on behind her back.

For another, she had already spent too much time listening to Frederick's dumb conversation. For a third, she did not want Darwin *flap-flap*ing around her bedroom and touching all her stuff. Most important of all, Mitzi felt she was being treated like a child, just because a real child happened to be present.

Mitzi was therefore amazed that Frederick, who was eleven, didn't resent being treated like a child too. In fact, Frederick seemed so eager to be with Mitzi that he led the way upstairs. Neither one of them cared that Darwin was stuck in the hallway below, unable to fit his dinosaur feet on the stairs.

"They're divorced, aren't they?" said Frederick.

"Who?" asked Mitzi.

"Your parents," said Frederick. "Your father divorced your mother and married someone else, didn't he?"

"Yes," said Mitzi, trying to remember. She hadn't seen her father for a long time.

"My mother is dead," said Frederick. "She died right after Darwin was born."

Mitzi sensed that Frederick thought it was much nicer to be dead than to be divorced and married to someone else.

"Grunch!" yelled the Tyrannosaurus Rex proudly. He had discovered that he could climb the stairs by sitting on his bottom and scooting up backwards. *Bump, bump,* he clamored after Frederick and Mitzi. *Bump, bump.*

"A husband should know that an archaeologist has to go off and work in the field," said Frederick. "Your father shouldn't have divorced her just because she went off in the summer to work in the field. I don't think it was Patricia's fault."

Mitzi was certain that her father was being insulted. Maybe her mother too. Frederick had no right to insult her parents, especially when he called them by the wrong names. "Her name is Pat," said Mitzi. "We use nicknames in our family."

"Not anymore," said Frederick. "My father doesn't allow nicknames."

Mitzi didn't care what Frederick's father allowed. He wasn't Mitzi's father. Maybe she should stop calling her mother Mom and start calling her Pat. Pat, Pat, Pat, she practiced silently.

Bump, bump, bump, came Darwin up the stairs, faster now that he had the hang of it.

"My wife will have to understand about fieldwork before we're married," said Frederick.

"Grunch!" said Darwin. He had triumphed over the entire staircase and was following Frederick and Mitzi down the hall to her bedroom. He headed straight for the miniature motorcycle collection on the bottom shelf of the bookcase.

"Don't touch those," Mitzi told him.

Removing his index finger from his mouth, Darwin picked up a Harley-Davidson. Mitzi pried it from his slobbery fingers and put it back on the shelf. "No one touches my motorcycles."

Darwin picked up a Yamaha.

Mitzi snatched it away and set it firmly on the bookcase. "No one touches my motorcycles!" she cried.

Frederick took the *D* volume of her encyclopedias from another shelf and set it on the floor. "Find the dinosaurs," he told Darwin.

Darwin squatted next to the book and began turning pages with moist fingers. At least he wasn't getting all that spit on her motorcycles.

"The only way to fight dinosaurs is with dinosaurs," Frederick explained. "Show Mitzi the triceratops."

Darwin obliged with a dark pink finger that made a damp splotch on Mitzi's book. Then he pointed to the brontosaurus and looked up at Mitzi with a grin. "That's you," he said. He really was kind of cute when he wasn't being a brat.

Darwin ducked his curly blond head close to the book and pretended to read. "Dinosaur is the familiar term for two extinct groups of reptiles."

Mitzi stared at him, astonished. She knew those hard words had been memorized, not read, but they were hard words nevertheless. Elsie Wolf's little sister could never have said them.

"We have the same encyclopedias at home," Frederick explained. "A bit grungier than yours, of course. You don't read much, do you?"

"I do too!" she raged. "All the time!"

Frederick shrugged. "I don't care how much you read."

Despite what he said, Mitzi could tell that Frederick was just like her mother. Mitzi's mother judged people by what books they read and how many hard words they knew.

"You're really hung up on motorcycles, aren't you?" Frederick asked.

"Motorcycles are my specialty," Mitzi admitted. She was proud of herself for remembering that hard word her mother had taught her this afternoon. *Specialty.* She must remember to say it again sometime.

"My father doesn't approve of motorcycles," said Frederick. "He thinks it should be against the law to sell them."

"Against the law?" Mitzi asked. She couldn't believe her ears.

"My father says motorcycles are as dangerous as cocaine and pot," Frederick explained. "If those things are against the law, motorcycles should be too."

A painful ball of worry lodged in Mitzi's chest, like bread and peanut butter she had eaten too fast. She hoped her mother wasn't really going to marry a man who believed motorcycles should be against the law.

"Did you draw these?" Frederick asked. He turned his head to include all the pictures of motorcycles on her walls. Black motorcycles, orange motorcycles, purple motorcycles, green motorcycles, all with lovely crayon rainbows behind them.

Mitzi nodded.

"I must say they're colorful," said Frederick. "The rainbows, I mean."

Mitzi was glad he had changed the subject. "Rainbows are my specialty, too," she said quickly and then wished she hadn't. Maybe Walter didn't like rainbows either.

"You're a good artist," Frederick said.

Another ache settled in Mitzi's chest. Frederick had sounded just like Mitzi's mother when he said that.

"Being a good artist is very important!" Mitzi argued. "Mrs. Fotheringham says so all the time! She always hangs my motorcycles and rainbows on the bulletin board."

"Did I say being an artist wasn't important?" Frederick asked.

"You were thinking it!" Mitzi accused. "You think I'm not living up to my potential just because I'd rather draw than read books or memorize stuff." She felt her chin quivering, so she turned her back. She never cried in front of strangers, especially dumb ones like Frederick.

"Is that what Patricia thinks?" Frederick asked.

"Yes," Mitzi said softly, remembering how empty and unappreciated she had felt at Christmas. She had drawn all these motorcycle pictures for her mother's Christmas present—secretly, at night, over many days and weeks. She had even wrapped them in red Christmas paper she bought at the store.

Mitzi had laid her gift proudly under the Christmas tree, confident that by Christmas night motorcycles would be racing on walls all over the house, even in her mother's study.

"You're a good artist," her mother had said. "Let's hang all these nice pictures in your bedroom where you can look at them."

Her mother didn't really think the pictures were nice, or she would have kept them herself. Frederick didn't like them either.

Maybe Mitzi shouldn't have drawn so many of them. Maybe she should have spent all that time drawing just one perfect motorcycle picture for her mother.

"I WANT THOSE!" cried Darwin, who was

standing beside Mitzi in striped stocking feet and pointing at her green ski boots.

"They're not yours," said Frederick. "It isn't polite to ask for things that don't belong to you. Don't give them to him," he told Mitzi.

"It's all right," said Mitzi. She was afraid her mother would say that a good hostess should always lend her ski boots to guests who asked for them. Besides, she was grateful for a reason to take them off. Her feet felt hot. They were smelly, too, she discovered as she removed the first one from its boot. Hurriedly Mitzi stepped out of both boots and put on her pink bedroom slippers.

"GRONCH!" said Darwin, very pleased with himself and his new brontosaurus feet. Mitzi noticed that he had changed his former *grunch* to match his newer and larger dinosaur personality. She also noticed that Darwin could not lift his newer and larger dinosaur feet. Maybe he would be stuck in her bedroom forever, a dinosaur as permanent as her window or the door to the hall.

"I don't exactly think motorcycles should be against the law," Frederick said. "But I've never been hung up on cars and motorcycles the way some kids are."

"Motorcycles are very complicated!" said Mitzi, defending her specialty. Ah! *Complicated.* She had said another hard word, without even planning it.

"Yeah, but they've never interested me," said Frederick. "I have a lot in common with Patricia."

Mitzi resented that. It didn't seem right for Frederick to have more in common with her mother than Mitzi did.

"You look like your father," she felt obliged to point out. Unlike Darwin, who was blue-eyed and blond, Frederick had dark hair and skin like Walter's. He would probably have hairy arms someday too.

"Yeah, but I don't act like him," said Frederick. "I'm not hung up on all the carpentry and yard work he does."

"What are you hung up on?" Mitzi asked angrily.

"Archaeology," said Frederick. "That's why Patricia is going to take me into the field with her this summer. She's going to teach me how to handle the screens."

The only field nearby was the one on University Street where Rosie the Doberman pinscher lived, and the lady who owned the house certainly wouldn't let Mitzi's mother go there. "My mother isn't going into the field," said Mitzi.

"Yes, she is," said Frederick. "In New Mexico. Hasn't she told you?"

Mitzi didn't know where New Mexico was.

Probably far away. Maybe they would have to stay overnight.

"It's all set," Frederick explained. "We're leaving on July 1, right after the honeymoon."

What honeymoon? Were they all going on a honeymoon together in a field? "You're going with us?" Mitzi asked.

"I'm going. You're staying here," said Frederick. "That's the only reason Patricia could start doing fieldwork again, because my father was willing to take care of you after they're married. It's really very nice of him, you know. Not all newlywed husbands would be willing to let their wives go off while they stay home and baby-sit."

"I don't want your father to baby-sit me!" Mitzi screamed.

Frederick remained calm. "I can understand why you might feel that way. But you're not old enough to go into the field and handle the screens. Maybe in a few years we'll take you. Besides, it's only for five weeks."

"Five weeks!" Mitzi yelled.

Frederick nodded pleasantly. "Don't feel bad. You've got your own tradeoffs. Nana is a better cook than your mother. You'll really like her meat loaf Wellington and banana cream pie."

"I like chicken from the Kentucky takeout!" cried Mitzi.

Frederick shrugged. "Suit yourself." He kicked off his shoes so he could stand on her bed and study another motorcycle picture. "You're really a terrific artist. You're the most terrific artist I know."

It infuriated Mitzi that he would say something nice to her in the middle of a quarrel. There was no way she could answer a compliment right now.

"What's your IQ?" he asked.

"I don't have one," Mitzi said crossly.

"I have a high IQ," butted in the dinosaur.

"Everyone has an IQ," explained Frederick. "It's the number for your intelligence quotient. It tells how smart you are."

"I'm eight," said Mitzi.

"That's your age, not your IQ," said Frederick. "You couldn't draw neat pictures like these if your IQ was only eight. I'm sure it's lots higher than that. At least over a hundred."

Mitzi considered that possibility. An IQ "over a hundred" sounded very impressive indeed. No wonder Mrs. Fotheringham was promoting her to the Red reading group.

Frederick lay back on the bed, his head resting on clasped hands. "I'm in the top five percent in our school, and I go to special classes for gifted kids. But I'm not good enough. I can't compete."

There was a bright kid in Mitzi's class who

could never hit a baseball. "Can't you play baseball?" she asked.

"Well, I'm not exactly our school's leading jock, but that doesn't bother me because I'm not hung up on sports. What I can't compete against is your average, ordinary, nonextinct dinosaur." Frederick pointed toward his brother with an elbow.

"You mean Darwin?" Mitzi was dumbfounded. "You're lots bigger than Darwin."

"Size is part of the problem, actually," explained Frederick. "I'm too big to be adorable."

Mitzi remembered how Nana Potts had cooed and called Darwin adorable when he'd been a brat and hadn't let Mitzi answer the telephone.

Frederick sighed. "The other part of my problem is that I'm only gifted. Darwin is a genius."

"He is not," said Mitzi. Darwin might be able to talk better than Elsie Wolf's little sister, but Mitzi was positive he was not a genius. "He didn't even know what *message* meant," she argued.

"Well, even geniuses aren't born with all the wisdom of the ages stuffed in their skulls. They have to learn things like everyone else. They just learn it faster."

"Maybe so," Mitzi acknowledged. "But Darwin isn't a genius."

"How many two-year-olds do you know who can read?" asked Frederick.

"None," said Mitzi. That was something else that she was positive about. No two-year-old in the whole world could read.

"Darwin is three now, but he's been reading for a long time," said Frederick. "We didn't even teach him. He just started picking up words by himself."

"I don't believe you," said Mitzi.

"WHAT ARE YOU HIDING?" Frederick suddenly yelled at his brother.

"Nothing," Darwin lied, stuffing something in his pocket and keeping his hand there to protect it.

"Give me that!" said Frederick. The brothers scuffled for a few seconds until Frederick won. "You little sneak! How many times have I told you that you can't just take things you want?" He handed a miniature Suzuki to Mitzi. "Tell Mitzi you're sorry you took her motorcycle."

Darwin said nothing. He hung his head and sucked his finger.

Mitzi examined the motorcycle to see that it was all right, then put it on a high shelf. She knew that any little kid who stole what he wanted wasn't smart enough to read.

"He wasn't reading that encyclopedia," she told Frederick. "He had just memorized the words. Lots of little kids can memorize words."

"I didn't say he could read encyclopedias,"

Frederick said. "But he can read almost any first or second or even third-grade book."

Mitzi knew that wasn't true. She was in the third grade, and Darwin couldn't read as well as she could. "No, he can't," she said.

"Do you want to bet?" Frederick challenged.

"Yes," she said.

"What will you bet?" Frederick asked.

She thought a minute. She had twenty-five cents in the old paper-clip box she kept in her underwear drawer. "Twenty-five cents."

"No, I want that red motorcycle picture," said Frederick, pointing to Mitzi's favorite one.

"Okay," said Mitzi. She wasn't afraid of losing it. "What do *you* bet?"

"Mmmm," said Frederick, thinking. "How about if I take your muddy shoes home and wash them for you before Patricia finds out?"

Mitzi beamed. Maybe Frederick wasn't really such an awful person. She held out her hand for him to shake.

"Okay," said Frederick. "Find me one of your schoolbooks, and I'll get Darwin to read it."

Mitzi looked anxiously about the room, then grabbed the book she had just brought home to read to her mother. There was no way that Darwin could read that hard book.

"I said he can read first or second or third-grade books," Frederick complained. "This is fourth-grade at least."

"No, it isn't. I'm in third grade, and my reading group has already read it." Mitzi hoped that God would not consider that a lie.

"The title is too hard for him," said Frederick. "He probably can't read the title."

"HAH!" said Mitzi.

Frederick opened the book and scanned it. "But the first page isn't very hard. He'll be able to read most of it."

Frederick strode over to Darwin, who had removed the brontosaurus feet to put a pair of Mitzi's ski gloves on his feet. Darwin waved his arms like a pterodactyl. "Grinch, grinch, grinch," he said happily.

"You're a grinch, all right," Frederick agreed. "Here, Darwin, show Mitzi how you can read this."

Darwin stuck his index finger in his mouth, plugging all words and further dinosaur sounds inside.

Frederick tried again. "Maybe there are some dinosaurs in this book."

Darwin looked tempted but didn't move.

Frederick held the book in front of his own face and pretended to read. "Wow! What a neat picture! Boy, I'll never let Darwin see this book."

Uncorking his mouth with a splatter of saliva, the dinosaur sprang. He leafed quickly through the pages with slobbery claws as Mitzi held her breath. She hoped Mrs. Fotheringham wouldn't notice the damage.

Darwin threw the book to the floor with disgust. "You tricked me."

"How do you know?" asked Frederick. "You didn't read it."

Darwin eyed the book suspiciously but picked it up.

"Read it," said Frederick.

No answer.

"Read it, you turkey," commanded Frederick.

"He can't read it," Mitzi cried. "I knew he couldn't. I win!"

"He could if he wanted to," Frederick complained.

"I win!" insisted Mitzi. She flopped on her stomach and reached under the bed.

"What are you doing?" Frederick asked.

"Getting a shopping bag. I don't want Mom to see you carrying my shoes to—"

She didn't finish her sentence. Behind her a small voice was speaking slowly and carefully: " 'How—would—you—like—to—live—in—a—home—that—had—only—one—door—and—no—windows?' "

Mitzi turned, stunned. Frederick was standing too far away. He wasn't prompting his brother.

Frederick reached for the picture of the red motorcycle. "I guess this is mine."

"Go on, take it!" cried Mitzi. "Take it!" Then she ran to Darwin and snatched Mrs. Fothering-ham's book from the terrible dinosaur's hands. "Give me that!" she screamed. "You're getting your filthy slobber all over my best schoolbook!"

Frederick smiled smugly. "I knew there would be sibling rivalry between you and Darwin. But you don't need to worry about me. You and I are going to get along okay."

4

Problems for Mitzi

Mitzi lay in bed, too full of *how come*'s to sleep. How come no one had felt sorry for her when Darwin wouldn't let her talk on her own telephone? How come the grown-ups thought Darwin was adorable just because he could read? How come no one around here noticed how spunky Mitzi was or cared that she was going to be promoted to the Red reading group?

And Frederick. How come he thought he was big enough to go into the field and handle screens for Mitzi's mother, whatever they were.

Through the window Mitzi could see the moon, which hung like a lonely pumpkin in the sky. What would happen to Mitzi if her mother married Walter? Mitzi was afraid that Walter would never notice her, let alone talk to her.

And what about her mother? Darwin was a little

genius who could read. Frederick was a future archaeologist who had lots in common with Mitzi's mother. With them around, her mother might forget about Mitzi.

Mitzi wanted to cry. When life got really terrible, she always felt better if she could cry. She squinched up her face. But the tears clung like thick syrup to her eyeballs and refused to flow down her cheeks in nice, comforting rivers. Nothing had gone right since she left school today. She had almost cried in front of Frederick, when she didn't want to. But now, when she did want to, she couldn't cry.

Mitzi tensed, hearing something. Was that her mother coming up the stairs? Yes, of course. She'd know those footsteps anywhere. Maybe her mother was so upset about the awful way the Potts family had acted at the party that she had decided not to marry Walter. Maybe her mother would take Mitzi to the field next summer to handle the screens.

Breathlessly Mitzi waited. Up the stairs came the footsteps. Down the hall. Then footsteps tiptoed to her bed.

"Mitzi," whispered her mother. "Are you asleep?"

"Aaah," said Mitzi, faking a yawn. "I'm a—wake."

Her mother sat on the bed and kissed her gently on the forehead. "Isn't it wonderful? Aren't you happy?"

Mitzi was feeling lots of things right now. But wonderful and happy weren't two of them.

"Frederick told me how much fun the two of you had together. He really likes you," her mother continued.

That big fibber, thought Mitzi.

"I'm glad the two of you hit it off so quickly. One of the reasons I wanted to get married again was so that you could be part of a real family. You're awfully silent, Miss Mitzi-Witzi," said her mother, calling her by the baby name she hadn't heard for a long time. "What are you thinking?"

"Nothing," said Mitzi. But she *was* thinking. Lots of things. She was thinking about their new picnic basket that didn't have enough plates and cups in it for all of Walter's family. She was thinking about how nicely she and her mother fit together on one Ferris wheel seat. She was thinking about the time she had her picture taken with her mother, just the two of them, for a Christmas card. She was thinking that she and her mother were already a real family.

"Well, that's a terrible scowl for someone who is thinking nothing," her mother said. "Come on. Out with it."

Mitzi scowled harder, wondering where to begin.

"If it's a big problem, maybe we can work it out together," her mother urged. "I'm listening."

"Frederick said you promised to take him into the field to handle the screens and not me," Mitzi blurted.

"Well," her mother said slowly. "He and I have talked about it. But I haven't promised anything definite yet."

Mitzi sat up in bed. "Take me instead!" she cried.

"Oh darling," said her mother, "you wouldn't enjoy handling the screens."

"Yes, I would!" Mitzi insisted. "What are they?"

Her mother smiled. Was she laughing at her? Mitzi didn't like being laughed at, especially right now.

"Well," said her mother, "archaeological screens are like the strainers you used to play with in your sandbox, except they're much bigger and heavier. Your arms would get tired if you had to work them. And you wouldn't like the heat either. The person on a dig who handles the screens has to stand in the hot sun all day, straining the dirt."

"How come?" Mitzi asked. Handling the

screens must be lots more fun than the way her mother was explaining it, or else Frederick wouldn't be so anxious to do it.

"Because there usually aren't many trees at an archaeological site. We always get up before sunrise and start working early in the morning. That means we can quit before the worst heat of the day in the late afternoon. But it still gets pretty hot sometimes."

"I mean how come you have to strain the dirt," Mitzi said.

"Well, sometimes the people doing the digging miss important objects like broken pieces of pottery. So someone else strains the dirt to make sure that nothing has been overlooked."

That didn't sound hard at all. Mitzi had strained lots and lots of sand in her lifetime. "I can do that!" She threw her arms around her mother. "Please take me with you!"

Her mother cradled Mitzi in her arms and rocked her gently back and forth. "Oh, Miss Mitzi-Witzi. Miss Mitzi-Witzi. I'll only be gone a few weeks. And Walter will be here to take care of you."

"Walter never talks to me," said Mitzi.

"I know he's awfully busy. But you'll have Nana Potts to talk to. And Darwin," said her mother.

Mitzi's mother didn't understand at all.

"Please take me instead of Frederick," Mitzi begged.

"Darling, you're only eight. Frederick has read lots of archaeology books," said her mother.

"I can read hard books now, too. I'm going to be in the Red reading group," said Mitzi.

"And I'm very proud of you," said her mother. "But Frederick wants to be an archaeologist when he grows up. He loves to study about Indians."

"Take both of us then," begged Mitzi. "I can learn about Indians. I'll show you!"

"Learning about Indians isn't the only thing you have to do before you go into the field. You have to prove you're grown up in other ways, too. But let's talk about this some other time, shall we?" suggested her mother. "It's past your bedtime." She gave Mitzi a kiss on the cheek and started for the door.

"Mom?" Mitzi called.

"Yes, dear?"

"I don't need a family. You don't have to marry Walter just for me," Mitzi said.

"I'm not doing it just for you, sweetheart," said her mother. "I'm doing it mostly for myself. I love him."

"Mom!" Mitzi cried.

"Yes, Mitzi," said her mother, less patiently.

"Walter thinks motorcycles should be against the law."

"Well," said her mother, "I'm sure he doesn't think your collection should be against the law. But if he does, I'll talk him out of it. Go to sleep now, dear. Good night."

Mitzi sighed as her mother walked out the door and down the hall. Mitzi still had lots of problems left to worry about—like how to persuade her mother to take her to the field. But at least she felt better about Walter and her motorcycle collection.

She turned over and closed her eyes, when suddenly another terrible thought struck her. She had to wash her yellow canvas shoes before her mother found them. Mitzi climbed out of bed and crept quietly to the door. She looked both ways to see if her mother was in sight. Then she walked carefully down the stairs to the utility room.

Mitzi's boot was exactly where she had left it: behind the washing machine. But where were her new yellow canvas shoes with blue stripes? Had her mother found them and decided to wash them? No, they weren't in the washer or in the dryer or on the utility room shelf. Had her mother already washed them and taken them upstairs? Mitzi raced back to her room to find out.

No, her shoes weren't in the closet. Mitzi herself could have dropped the shoes separately, almost anywhere. But if her mother had taken them to Mitzi's room, they would be sitting side by side, like matched canaries, pointing toward the closet wall. Had her mother hidden her wonderful new shoes to punish her for getting them muddy?

All the peace that Mitzi had felt a few minutes earlier was gone. She climbed into bed and pulled the covers over her head so she wouldn't have to look at the lonely March moon.

5

Found and Lost

Mitzi tried to act like a Red when she left her classroom Monday afternoon. Now that she was in the best reading group, she shouldn't act anxious to go home from school. She shouldn't just yank her parka off the hook and start running. She should stop in the hall and slowly put her coat on, zipping it all the way up to her chin the way Felicia Stewart did.

While she was zipping, Mr. Ledgard walked over.

"Hi there, Mitzi," said the janitor. "I've been looking for you all day. Didn't you get my message?"

"What message?" asked Mitzi, astonished. This had been a very exciting day. First Mrs. Fotheringham had sent Mitzi on an errand to the supply room with Felicia Stewart. Now Mr. Ledgard, the most important person in the whole school, was trying to give her a message.

"How did the reading go?" asked Mr. Ledgard. "Did you get promoted?"

"Fine. Yes," said Mitzi. "What message?" she repeated.

"I left a message with your little brother," said Mr. Ledgard. "Didn't he tell you?"

"I don't have any brother," said Mitzi.

"Funny," said Mr. Ledgard, slowly shaking his head. "He acted like he was your brother. He was just a little tyke, though. Maybe he didn't understand me. Guess I called up the wrong number."

"Oh!" groaned Mitzi, suddenly understanding. She wasn't in the Red group for nothing. "You talked to Darwin. He's just some little boy my mother knows. What did you want me for?"

"Well, I called you up cause I didn't want you to worry none about that boot you lost," said Mr. Ledgard.

Mitzi brightened. "You found my boot?"

"Yep," said Mr. Ledgard. "Knew it was yours soon as I seen it. Figured Rosie must have stole it while you was walking home. She's always running off with my work gloves."

"Oh, thank you! Where did you find it?" she asked.

"Behind the shed at the Lewis place. I work for Mrs. Lewis after school, when I can, and most Saturdays," Mr. Ledgard explained.

"Oh," said Mitzi, less happily. "Is it still there?" She wasn't sure she wanted to go back to Mrs. Lewis's house, even with Mr. Ledgard.

"It's right down the hall in my room. We can go get it now if you want," Mr. Ledgard suggested.

Of course Mitzi wanted to go. It was a great honor to walk down the hall with Mr. Ledgard and go in his room. Mitzi waved cheerily to Felicia Stewart and her friends so they would be sure to notice.

"Here you go," said Mr. Ledgard, handing her the boot.

"Thank you," said Mitzi. But she was looking at something more interesting. On Mr. Ledgard's shelf were two miniature motorcycles.

"Oh," said Mitzi. "Do you collect miniature motorcycles?"

"Yep," said Mr. Ledgard. "But I like real ones better."

"Real ones?" Mitzi squealed. "Do you have some real motorcycles?"

"Just one," said Mr. Ledgard. "But it's pretty spiffy. It has a sidecar."

"What's a sidecar?" Mitzi asked.

"Oh, it's a seat on wheels that fits on the side,"

said Mr. Ledgard. "I bought it so's I could take people for rides with me. Some folks won't get on a motorcycle, you know."

Mitzi couldn't imagine anyone not wanting to get on a motorcycle, especially with Mr. Ledgard. How wonderful it would be to have a father like Mr. Ledgard who took you for motorcycle rides! Not one like Walter, who thought motorcycles should be against the law.

She was thinking about how she might introduce her mother to Mr. Ledgard when she noticed a picture on the shelf. It showed Mr. Ledgard with an old lady. "Is that your mother?" Mitzi asked.

"Nope. That's me and my wife Ellie on our forty-third wedding anniversary last month."

"Oh," said Mitzi, feeling like a glass of root beer that has lost its fizz. She hadn't been too hopeful that her mother could be persuaded to marry Mr. Ledgard instead of Walter. But this news about a Mrs. Ledgard seemed to settle the matter. "That's a nice frame," she added lamely.

"Making picture frames is one of my hobbies," said Mr. Ledgard.

"You made this neat frame?" Mitzi asked, impressed.

"Yep. I like to design frames to match the pictures that go in them. It makes the pictures look real special," he explained.

"Yes," said Mitzi, not really agreeing. She didn't think the old lady in the picture looked so special. Not nearly as special as her own mother. But she knew it wouldn't be polite to say so. "Well, I guess I better be going. My mother gets worried when I don't come straight home from school."

"It's getting late, all right," said Mr. Ledgard. "But you come back and visit me again sometime. Hear?"

"Yeah, I will. All the time," Mitzi offered. "Thanks for finding my boot."

"You're welcome," said Mr. Ledgard. "Good-bye now."

"'Bye," said Mitzi. She ran down the hall to the door, forgetting until she got there that Felicia Stewart never ran in the halls.

After such an exciting day at school, she almost even forgot that her mother was planning to marry Walter. She was startled to see Frederick in her house when she arrived home. He was sitting in the dining room, talking to Mitzi's mother about Navaho poetry.

Frederick jumped up at once. "Hey, I've been waiting for you," he told Mitzi. "Can we go up to your room and talk a minute?"

"I guess so," said Mitzi doubtfully. She didn't like the strange way he was acting or the suspicious way his coat bulged. Well, he better not think he could play any tricks on her now that she was a Red and living up to her potential.

When they were alone in Mitzi's room, Frederick removed a paper bag from under his coat and shoved it in Mitzi's stomach.

"Here. I washed these for you," said Frederick.

"Oh boy! Thanks!" cried Mitzi, opening the bag. Her yellow canvas shoes looked bright as new.

"I know I won the bet and I didn't have to wash them," said Frederick. "But I decided it was the least I could do for you, under the circumstances."

"Huh?" said Mitzi. Why didn't Frederick ever talk in words she could understand?

"It seemed appropriate to do something nice for you to make up for the fact that Patricia is going to take me into the field this summer to handle the screens," he explained.

Frederick looked so smart-alecky Mitzi wanted to scream.

"I'm going with Mom too," she blurted.

"Did she change her mind?" Frederick asked.

"Well, she will!" Mitzi said.

"No she won't," he replied. "But I guess I

wouldn't mind too much if she did. Well, I've got to go. See you."

As he darted down the hall, Mitzi slammed her bedroom door. She stood against it, shaking with anger and self-pity.

6

A Daring Decision

Spring winds came and, afterwards, daffodils. Then in late April something else came to Mitzi's house. Walter. He arrived in blue jeans, carrying pencils and rulers, and he spent the day measuring her utility room and back porch. From then on he came regularly, bringing saws and hammers and, unfortunately, Darwin.

After each visit, Mitzi found new damage Tyrannosaurus Rex had caused—chocolate milk on her Snoopy pillow, bubble gum on her stuffed monkey, and red Magic Marker on three of her miniature motorcycles!

At school, however, life for Mitzi took an important new direction. She became Mr. Ledgard's self-appointed assistant, sometimes even staying after school to empty wastebaskets and carry sweaters to the Lost and Found. Everyone was jealous, even Felicia Stewart.

One Friday morning in May, Mitzi arrived at school early enough to drop by Mr. Ledgard's room and say hello before the bell rang. Mitzi gasped when she opened the door. A man, who didn't look at all like Mr. Ledgard, was sprawled in his chair, smoking a cigarette.

"Don't you kids ever knock?" the man asked.

"Where's Mr. Ledgard?" asked Mitzi.

"He's taking the day off," said the man and blew a puff of smoke in her direction.

Mitzi, who did not like cigarette smoke, coughed. "How come?" she demanded.

"He has a backache or something. How should I know? Hey, kid, beat it, will you? I have work to do."

Mitzi's mouth fell open. No grown-up had ever talked to her like that. Even the grumpy school crossing guards didn't usually talk to her like that. Startled, she did exactly as she was told and beat it out the door.

Standing in the hall, Mitzi thought about *beat it.* Maybe beating it wasn't such a bad idea. Maybe she should beat it to Mr. Ledgard's house. Sick people needed visitors.

But before she could beat it to Mr. Ledgard's house, she would have to go home and ask for a ride. Her mother would find Mr. Ledgard's address in the phone book.

That decision made, she walked through the

hall, opened the door, and ran across the playground. How brave she was! She had never skipped school before, not even on her birthday.

The closer Mitzi got to her home, however, the more she wondered if she were doing the right thing. What would her mother say? Mitzi's mother did not believe in skipping school. Would she make Mitzi go right back again? Even worse, would she ground Mitzi over the weekend?

Mitzi was certainly not prepared for the way her mother greeted her. "Oh, Mitzi, I'm so glad you're home. You're not sick, are you?"

"No, but Mr. Ledgard is. He didn't come to school today. I have to go see him," Mitzi explained.

"Well, I'm glad you're here. A terrible problem just came up. I need you to watch Darwin."

"Darwin!" wailed Mitzi. Darwin was the last thing she wanted to watch.

BONNNG! came a noise from under the table where Darwin was playing with the beautiful brass dinner gong.

Mitzi gasped. Frederick had been allowed to strike the gong once, at the party, to call everyone to dinner. But it was unthinkable that Darwin could sit and play with the gong that Mitzi was not allowed to touch.

"Look what Darwin is doing," Mitzi felt obliged

to tell her mother. Her mother didn't look up. She was busy stuffing papers into a briefcase.

BONNNG! went the gong.

Mitzi had seldom been this close to the gong. She looked at the mallet Darwin was clutching and longed to hold it in her own hand.

"Shall I play a song for you?" Mitzi asked.

Darwin shook his head.

"Here, I'll show you," Mitzi offered. She reached for the mallet.

"GRUNCH!" yelled the dinosaur.

Mitzi's mother swooped down on the gong and mallet like a hungry eagle and set them above reach. "Walter should be here soon," she explained. "He just went to the lumber mill to buy a few things. He's so anxious to get Mother Potts' bedroom finished that he took the day off from the university to work on it. I told Walter I'd keep an eye on Darwin while I graded papers, but I just got a phone call. I have to attend a special meeting."

"Why can't Walter's mother watch Darwin?" Mitzi complained.

"Her sister is in town, and they've gone shopping together."

Mitzi was busy today too. "I can't watch Darwin," she said. "I have to see Mr. Ledgard. I told you—he's sick."

"Oh! What a shame. Well, I'll drive you there

when I get back. Or you can ask Walter to take you, if you don't want to wait for me. I've got to run. I'm already late for my meeting." She started toward the door.

"Mom?"

"Yes, Mitzi?"

"I'd like to take Mr. Ledgard a get-well present. Do you have a present I can take him?" Mitzi asked.

"I want a present," said Darwin, crawling out from under the table.

"Well, maybe we can buy him some flowers tomorrow," said her mother.

"I want to take him a present today," said Mitzi.

"I want a present today," echoed Darwin.

"Why don't you make him a card with some felt-tip pens?" suggested Mitzi's mother. "You can give some paper to Darwin and keep him entertained until Walter comes. Call Mrs. Howard next door if you have any problems." She kissed both children on the tops of their heads. "Good-bye."

As soon as the door shut, Darwin pointed to the dinner gong on the high shelf. "Grunch!" he demanded.

"You can't have it," said Mitzi.

Darwin stamped a blue tyrannosaurus rex foot. "GRUNCH!"

"It won't do you any good to yell," said Mitzi. "Mom won't let me play with it either."

Darwin climbed under the table and sucked his finger, looking up at Mitzi with sad blue eyes.

"Let's draw pictures until Walter comes," she coaxed.

Mitzi got a big stack of paper from her mother's desk drawer and the plastic case of felt-tip pens, wondering what kind of a card to draw for Mr. Ledgard. She tried to remember all the best cards she had ever received—a valentine with a bear holding heart-shaped balloons, a birthday card with a girl blowing out eight candles, a postcard of the Golden Gate Bridge. None of them seemed right for Mr. Ledgard, who, she remembered with pleasure, rode a motorcycle with a sidecar.

Yes, of course. She would draw Mr. Ledgard a motorcycle. Motorcycles were Mitzi's specialty.

Sidecars, however, were not her specialty. Mitzi had never seen a sidecar, not even Mr. Ledgard's. He drove a yellow Toyota to school. Mitzi wondered briefly if sidecars looked like yellow Toyotas but decided not to risk it.

Instead, she worked on a plain black motorcycle while Darwin filled all the other papers with creatures that looked like pumpkins on stork legs. Each one smiled with a huge mouth full of pointy teeth, and under each one he had printed DARWIN THE TERRIBLE.

"Those are nice pumpkins," Mitzi told him.

"Grunch," said Darwin with a snarl that showed off his own little white teeth.

"Oh," said Mitzi, understanding. "I mean those are nice tyrannosaurus rexes."

Mitzi looked at the clock. Walter had not come home "soon." Walter had not come home in nearly an hour. Mitzi was getting tired of watching Darwin.

"I'm hungry," said Darwin. "I want a cookie."

Mitzi went to the bread box and found him one.

"Oh boy! Oreos!" exclaimed Darwin. "We have to eat homemade cookies at our house." He pulled it apart and licked the frosting.

The phone rang, and Darwin sprang after it.

"I'll get it," he said.

"NO, YOU WON'T!" Mitzi screamed, remembering how he answered phones. "Hello?"

"Mitzi?" said Walter. "Where's Patricia?"

"She had to go to a meeting," Mitzi explained.

"Did she take Darwin?" Walter asked.

"No. I'm watching him until you get here. When are you coming?"

"I've been to two lumber mills and haven't found what I need," said Walter. "I may be another couple of hours."

"Another couple of hours!" wailed Mitzi. "I'm supposed to go to Mr. Ledgard's house. What can I do with Darwin?"

"Who's Mr. Ledgard?" asked Walter.

"My best friend. He works at our school."

"Why don't you take Darwin with you?" Walter suggested pleasantly. He probably didn't want to watch the dinosaur either.

"I need you to help me," complained Mitzi. "I don't know how to look up addresses in the phone book."

There was some mumbling on the other end of the line, as if Walter were talking to someone else.

"Sorry, Mitzi," Walter said, very businesslike. "I've got to hang up now. Someone needs to use the phone. Good-bye."

The receiver clicked.

7

The Wagon Ride

Mitzi sighed as she hung up the receiver after talking to Walter.

Then Darwin paddled over to her on his blue swim fins. "*I* know how to look up addresses in the phone book," he bragged.

"So?" she said rudely. Mitzi's mother did not like her to say "so."

"It's easy. I'll show you," he said.

Mitzi looked at Darwin doubtfully. Geniuses were not to be trusted. Maybe—just maybe—he was offering to help her. But more likely he was trying to play some kind of trick. "How?" she challenged.

"You look it up under the last name," said Darwin.

"His name is Ledgard," said Mitzi.

"How do you spell it?" Darwin asked.

"It begins with *L,*" said Mitzi. She closed her

eyes and tried to figure out the rest. *"L-E-D-G-A-R-D."*

What the heck, thought Mitzi. It couldn't hurt to try. She opened the phone book and read the first name she saw. It wasn't one she was familiar with, so she pronounced the words slowly. "Redmond, Da-vid."

"*L* comes before *R,*" said Darwin, helping her with messy Oreo fingers. It took a long time, but they finally found Ledgard. Luckily, there was only one Ledgard in the phone book.

Mitzi's mood went from pleasure to disappointment as she read the address aloud. "1224 Cloverdale Road. I don't know where Cloverdale Road is," she admitted.

"I do," said Darwin. "Nana goes to the beauty parlor on Cloverdale Road. She takes me with her."

Mitzi's eyes widened. "Can you show me how to get there?"

"Yep," said Darwin, and then added, "but I won't."

"You won't!" cried Mitzi. "How come?"

Darwin lifted an awkward blue tyrannosaurus rex foot for her to see. "Dinosaurs don't like to walk."

"Didn't you bring any shoes with you?" Mitzi asked disgustedly.

Darwin shook his head.

"How about if I pull you in my wagon?" Mitzi suggested, remembering the wonderful old toy from some foreign country. It was lower and narrower than American wagons, but big enough for Darwin.

Darwin thought about that but shook his head again. "No," he said. He started to suck his finger but got a better idea for something to put in his mouth. "I want another cookie."

Mitzi ignored the request. "Why won't you show me?" she demanded.

"Grunch," said Tyrannosaurus Rex, deciding to suck his finger after all.

"WHY NOT?" she yelled. "And if you say 'grunch' again I won't give you anything to eat all day!"

Raindrops seemed to appear in Darwin's innocent eyes, and he pulled his finger from his mouth. "I'm hungry."

"Okay," suggested Mitzi. "If I make you a peanut butter sandwich and give you two Oreos and pull you in the wagon, will you show me how to get to Cloverdale Road?"

Darwin screwed up his face to think about that. "No," he said.

"Please," said Mitzi sweetly.

"No," said Darwin.

"But I said the magic word," she pointed out.

Darwin grinned. "Didn't work, did it?"

In spite of herself, Mitzi grinned back. "How about if I make you a peanut butter sandwich and give you the whole package of Oreos to eat while we go?" she bargained.

Darwin considered that. "Okay," he agreed at last.

With Darwin finally inside her old weather-beaten wagon, Mitzi made sure the other things were aboard, too—peanut butter sandwiches for both of them, the package of cookies for Darwin, and the motorcycle picture for Mr. Ledgard, carefully rolled up in a rubber band.

Squeak, squeak, went the wagon as she pulled it from the garage to the sidewalk. Wondering where to go next, Mitzi turned around to ask Darwin. He had ripped a sandwich apart to eat the peanut butter off the top of the bread, and there were brown blobs on his nose and chin. "Which way?" Mitzi asked.

"Grunch!" said Darwin, pointing with half a sandwich. *Squeak, squeak, squeak, squeak, squeak.* On and on they went, Mitzi pulling, Darwin eating and pointing, the wagon squeaking.

The sun grew hotter, and Mitzi grew more tired. Nothing looked familiar, and a dark thought crossed her mind. What if Darwin didn't really know where Cloverdale Road was? What if he could find Cloverdale Road from his own house but not from hers? What if he was just playing a trick on her? She forced herself to think about Mr. Ledgard and how pleased he would be to see her.

But the load seemed to grow heavier and heavier. Finally Mitzi could not pull the wagon at all. She turned around and saw that Darwin was pointing up. "See! I told you I could find it!" he bragged.

The sign said CLOVERDALE ROAD.

Grateful to Darwin for guiding them to safety, Mitzi felt irritated as well. How come he always thought he knew more than she did? I can read too, thought Mitzi, who wished it had occurred to her earlier to look up at the street signs. Well, she wouldn't ask him any more questions. From here on, she would find Mr. Ledgard's house without any more help from that know-it-all.

"What's on that motorcycle?" asked Darwin, climbing out of the wagon and *flap-flap*ing to a strange piece of machinery parked in the driveway.

"I don't know," Mitzi started to say and then decided she did know. Of course she knew!

"That's a sidecar," she said, proud to tell Darwin something he didn't know.

She walked around it in amazement. A sidecar

didn't look like anything she had imagined. Could this be where Mr. Ledgard lived? Sure enough, the number on the house said 1224.

As Mitzi rang the doorbell, she felt a sharp pain on her bottom. Darwin had smacked her.

"MAKE THEM HURRY UP!" he howled. "I HAVE TO GO TO THE BATHROOM!"

8

Mr. Ledgard's Motorcycle

Mitzi was doing something she had dreamed of all her life. Mitzi was riding on a motorcycle. She was riding behind Mr. Ledgard, holding him tightly about the waist as the wind prickled her skin and flung her hair. And who did Mitzi have to thank for making this glorious experience possible? That dumb Darwin, that's who.

While Mr. Ledgard was thanking her for the picture she'd drawn, Mitzi had looked at the motorcycle hungrily. But Darwin had just pointed at the sidecar and said, "I want to ride in that!"

Mr. Ledgard had carefully wedged Mitzi's wagon into the sidecar beside Darwin. Now here they were. Darwin waved at a repairman standing on a yellow truck ladder. The man waved back so cheerily that Mitzi waved too. Flying on the back of an eagle, or even the back of an angel, couldn't be as dizzying as sailing along the city streets on Mr. Ledgard's motorcycle.

Up and down hills, along straight stretches, over bridges and through tunnels they *vroom*ed. At last Mr. Ledgard pulled up in Mitzi's driveway and stopped.

"Well, I guess that's enough for one day," said Mr. Ledgard, removing the wagon from the side-car. "I feel a lot better now. That did my back a lot of good."

Mitzi understood perfectly. A motorcycle ride was the best medicine in the whole world.

Mitzi thanked her friend for the wonderful ride. Then she followed Darwin into Nana Potts' future bedroom, where Walter was hammering.

"I'm not a tyrannosaurus rex anymore," Darwin announced.

"That's nice," said Walter absently, without looking up. "Now maybe you can wear shoes to the wedding."

Darwin picked up a rag from his father's work-table and put it on his head. "I'm going to wear a helmet to the wedding. I'm a motorcycle driver like Mr. Ledgard." He held out two fists and worked them back and forth. "Vroom! Vroom!"

"That's nice," said Walter again, lifting his arm. *Bam! Bam! Bam!* went his hammer.

"He took us on his motorcycle," Darwin offered.

Walter suddenly stopped hammering and looked at Darwin. "Did he give you motorcycle helmets to wear?"

"He tried to, but they didn't fit," said Darwin. "I want a motorcycle helmet."

"Where did you go on the motorcycle?" Walter asked, strangely interested.

"All over," said Darwin. "Mitzi rode on the seat with Mr. Ledgard, but I got to ride in the sidecar. I want a helmet like Mr. Ledgard's and a motorcycle collection like Mitzi's."

Walter set down his hammer and took Mitzi firmly by her shoulders. "Don't you know how dangerous motorcycles are? The two of you could have been killed or maimed for life. Don't you ever do that again."

Walter doesn't know anything, thought Mitzi. She knew that Mr. Ledgard would never let her or Darwin get hurt. She stood there wondering how to explain to Walter about what a gentle man Mr. Ledgard was, and how exciting the motorcycle ride had been.

But she couldn't put her thoughts about Mr. Ledgard together because she was also busy thinking about something else. Walter had actually looked at her and touched her and talked to her as if she were a real person.

Now that was something to think about!

9

The Indian War

"From beneath the life-giving sun—" recited Mitzi.

With the help of Frederick and her mother, Mitzi was trying to learn her part for the wedding ceremony. It was taking a long time, mainly because she had to learn a crummy poem with words that didn't make any sense.

Through the open window of her mother's bedroom, they could hear Nana Potts arguing with the gardener.

"Having the garden planted properly is my wedding gift to the bride and groom," said Nana Potts, whose sugary voice had turned shrill. "I ordered two hundred pink geraniums, not two hundred red geraniums. Red geraniums just don't look weddingy."

In Mitzi's opinion, nothing about her mother's

marriage to Walter was turning out to be very weddingy. Mitzi, who had attended three of them, was an expert on real weddings.

Real weddings took place in churches, with organ music and bridesmaids in pretty dresses and ministers who read from the Bible. They did not take place in ordinary backyards with Frederick playing the accordion or a lady judge performing the ceremony.

And this was the worst part. Real weddings did not have a program where the bride's daughter recited an Indian poem, which wasn't even a real Indian poem but just some dumb words made up by plain old Frederick.

"Go on with the poem," said Mitzi's mother.

"Life-giving sun," Mitzi repeated, stalling for time. She couldn't remember the next stupid line.

His head packaged in Frederick's red football helmet, Darwin came chugging into the room. "Vroom, vroom, vroom," said the former Tyrannosaurus Rex, working his fists back and forth.

"Go on, Mitzi," said her mother.

"Life-giving sun—life-giving sun—" Mitzi stammered.

"From beneath the life-giving sun, From beneath the strength-giving rain," prompted the motorcycle rider.

They all turned to stare at Darwin, even Frederick.

"How did you know that?" Frederick demanded.

"Those are the words I heard you saying in your room," said Darwin. "I listened through the closet. What's life-giving sun?" he asked Mitzi's mother.

"The sun gives life to the world because it makes the plants grow that all the animals and people eat," explained her mother. "That's the way the Navahos talk. Frederick and I thought it would be nice to have a Navaho wedding poem at your father's and my wedding."

"How come?" asked Darwin.

"Because Patricia is an archaeologist," said Frederick loudly, settling the matter.

"My specialty is Indians of the Southwest," Mitzi's mother explained. "So Frederick composed an Indian poem for Mitzi to recite at the wedding."

"I want to be an Indian at the wedding," said Darwin.

"You can't," said Frederick. "I wrote the poem for Mitzi."

"I know it better than she does," Darwin argued, and he began reciting. He went through all thirteen lines without missing a syllable.

Frederick remained staunch. "Mitzi can do it better than you can. Show him, Mitzi."

Mitzi held up her chin and began confidently, remembering the lines Darwin had just recited. "From beneath the life-giving sun, From beneath the strength-giving rain, Here upon Mother Earth, We stand in peace, In a—"

Darwin grinned triumphantly from under the red football helmet. "You said it wrong. We stand in *time,* not *peace.* I get to be the Indian."

"Maybe we could divide the poem so both of them could be on the program," Mitzi's mother suggested.

Frederick looked pained. "That would spoil everything!"

"I WANT TO BE THE INDIAN!" Darwin howled.

"Maybe we should let him do it," said Mitzi's mother. "Mitzi told me she didn't want to take part in the wedding unless she could be a flower girl, but I was hoping she'd feel better about the poem after she learned it."

Mitzi felt double-crossed. It wasn't nice of her mother to fink on her to Frederick about something she had said in private, and at least two days ago. People could change their minds, couldn't they?

"Darwin will just louse things up at the last

minute," complained Frederick. "Besides, he always gets his own way."

"I do not," said Darwin. "Everybody's doing something at the wedding but me. I want to be the Indian." Tears came gushing down his cheeks. "I know the poem better than Mitzi."

"Well, Mitzi?" asked her mother.

"Okay, let Darwin be on the program if he wants to," said Mitzi, feeling virtuous and grown-up, but at the same time awkward and miserable. Even though Mitzi was keeping peace by giving Darwin his own way, she had the feeling that she hadn't lived up to her potential. Maybe she should have tried harder to learn Frederick's stupid poem. Maybe no one would notice her at the wedding if she didn't have a job to do.

Mitzi went to her bedroom and shut the door. Mindlessly she sat down at her desk and began doodling on an old note pad with some felt-tip pens. She studied her scribbles—a row of colored circles with crossed lines inside like motorcycle spokes. Then she rumpled the paper, got out a nice big sheet, and began to work in earnest.

The resulting picture was different from any she had ever made. She had never drawn a motorcycle with a sidecar before, or even a motorcycle with a passenger. But this new drawing showed three passengers—Mr. Ledgard in his helmet,

Mitzi hugging him tightly around the waist, and Darwin in the sidecar, waving to a repairman on the ladder of a yellow truck.

Mitzi knew the picture was good—so good she wanted more than anything to give it to her mother and Walter for a wedding present. But would her mother just give it back again, suggesting they hang it in Mitzi's room? Would Walter give it back, saying he didn't approve of motorcycles?

Mitzi was worrying about those things when her mother knocked gently on the door. "Mitzi? May I come in?"

Mitzi nervously turned the picture facedown and leaned an elbow on it. "Yeah," she answered.

Her mother pulled up another chair and sat down beside her. "Honey, I know that so far this wedding hasn't been very much fun for you. Weddings should be happy days for everyone involved, not just for the bride and groom. I especially want you to be happy on my wedding day."

Mitzi wiggled her toes inside her socks. She hadn't had a nice talk like this with her mother for a long time. Surely her mother was going to say that Darwin was too little to recite a poem at her wedding and that a grown-up, responsible girl like Mitzi should do it. Instead, her mother pulled a white envelope from the pocket of her jeans.

"I thought you might enjoy the wedding more if you could invite your very own guest to sit next to. Why don't you take this invitation to Elsie Wolf and tell her we'd love to have her come to the wedding?"

"Oh," said Mitzi, disappointed that the conversation had taken an unexpected turn. "Elsie's out of town. Her family left on vacation as soon as school was out last week."

"Well, maybe you can think of someone else you'd like to invite. I'll leave this invitation here for you, just in case." Her mother kissed Mitzi on the cheek and left the room.

Staring at the white envelope, Mitzi suddenly had a great idea. In fact, she suddenly had two great ideas. She rolled up her new motorcycle picture and put a rubber band around it, grabbed the invitation, and rushed downstairs.

10

Mitzi's Happy Day

Nana Potts had been right about one thing. The garden did look weddingy with two hundred pink geraniums planted in it.

The day before the ceremony a stream of people kept bringing other stuff too. Men from U-Rental huffed to the backyard, carrying white folding chairs and round tables. A lady from the department store brought colored tablecloths and ribbon streamers. Florist helpers shuffled in and out, balancing arrangements of fresh carnations and daisies. Mitzi's house became so interesting that secretly she was pleased her mother and Walter were being married in the garden instead of at a church, like a real bride and groom.

Best of all, the day of the wedding a crew came from the caterers. They filed into the kitchen with amazing kinds of hot and cold treats, including a rainbow of miniature French pastries.

Just to make sure that all the pastries were nice enough to serve at a wedding, Mitzi sampled two of them and was reaching for a third when she felt something grab her arm.

"Haven't we eaten enough?" asked Nana Potts, who lately was beginning to appear out of nowhere, when Mitzi least expected her. "Let's not eat any more until the guests have had a turn, shall we?"

Besides showing up when she wasn't wanted, Nana Potts had started calling Mitzi *we.*

"Okay," said Mitzi, who didn't want to spill on her new dress anyway. She strolled into the front hallway, where there wasn't much furniture to bump into, and began to twirl.

Mitzi twirled and twirled until the ruffly skirt of her new white dress stood straight out at the sides. Of all the new things they had purchased for the ceremony, Mitzi's new dress was certainly the most weddingy, and Mitzi was very proud of it. She just wished her mother had chosen one more like it, instead of that purple thing with the straight skirt. The truth was that Mitzi did not think her mother's dress looked very much like a bride's, but Mitzi was too polite to mention it.

"Oh, Mitzi," said her mother, bending down to kiss her. "You look beautiful enough to eat."

"You look beautiful too," said Mitzi, who

wasn't really lying. Except for the fact that her mother didn't look much like a bride, she looked very pretty. Mitzi especially liked the way her mother's hair was arranged on her head with a cluster of purple flowers that smelled like fresh fruit.

"You're as happy as I am, aren't you?" said her mother with a squeeze.

Happy? wondered Mitzi. She knew she was excited. But she wasn't sure that *excited* and *happy* meant the same thing.

Her mother held her arms around Mitzi, rubbing her chin in Mitzi's hair. "It's going to be fun for all of us to belong to a wonderful big family." Then her mother stood up abruptly. "You never told me if you invited anyone to the wedding."

Mitzi hadn't told her on purpose. She wanted her guests to be a surprise.

"Well," said her mother. "Did you invite someone?"

"Yes," said Mitzi, not wanting to explain just yet.

"Who?" insisted her mother.

Mitzi smoothed a wrinkle from her mother's dress. "Mr. and Mrs. Ledgard."

"Mr. and Mrs. Ledgard?" said her mother with a grin. Mitzi hoped her mother was smiling with pleasure, but she wasn't quite sure.

"Well," said her mother, "I'm sure you'll be a good hostess. You better go outside to the garden and watch for them. The guests are starting to arrive."

"Aren't you coming?" Mitzi asked.

"The bride isn't supposed to appear until everyone is seated. Run along now." Mitzi started to leave, but her mother called her back. "How about a kiss for luck?"

After they had a good squeeze, Mitzi went outside. She found Mrs. Ledgard examining one of the two hundred pink geraniums. Mr. Ledgard carried a package tied in white tissue paper, and he was wearing a blue plaid polyester suit. Mitzi had never seen him so dressed up before and decided he looked very handsome in a necktie.

"Hi," she said, rubbing her finger along the package he was holding. "I hope Mom and Walter like their present."

"You bet they'll like it," Mr. Ledgard assured her. "It's right spiffy looking, if I do say so myself."

Some of the guests were already seated on the folding chairs, waiting for the ceremony, so Mitzi found places for herself and the Ledgards on the first row.

"MR. LEDGARD!" shrieked Darwin, running to greet him. Darwin was wearing a red sweatband with a yellow feather stuck in it. Frederick, trailing a few paces behind his brother, was wearing a martyred expression.

Mitzi turned to Frederick. "What's he doing with that dumb feather in his hair? He'll spoil the wedding!"

"I've been trying to get it away from him," said Frederick. "But you know Darwin. He thinks he's Marlon Brando."

"I do not! I think I'm an Indian," said Darwin.

"Same thing," said Frederick.

"Ugh!" said Darwin, folding his arms stiffly in front of him.

"How many times do I have to tell you that real Indians don't say 'ugh'?" complained Frederick. "Especially Navahos."

"I'm an Indian, and I say 'ugh'!" argued Darwin. "Ugh, ugh, ugh!"

Frederick was bored with his brother. "Mitzi and Darwin have told me all about you, Mr. Ledgard. They say you have a neat motorcycle."

"I want to go for a ride on your motorcycle," said Darwin.

"Sorry, not today," said Mr. Ledgard. "Didn't bring it."

"We didn't think it was fancy enough for a wedding," said Mrs. Ledgard.

Darwin was stunned. *"You didn't bring it!"*

"Hey, pipe down, will you?" ordered Frederick. "Everybody's staring at you."

"I want to go for a motorcycle ride," demanded Darwin, shoving an empty folding chair so it crashed to the ground.

"You turkey!" Frederick grumbled. "Why don't you act your age? Why don't you ever act your age?"

"HE DIDN'T BRING HIS MOTORCYCLE, DARN HIM!" roared the Indian.

"Will you shut up?" growled Frederick.

"Come on now, boys," said Nana Potts, who had done her magic act of appearing out of the air. "We don't want to spoil our daddy's wedding day, do we? Frederick, it's time for you to get your accordion and start the program. Darwin, you come sit with Nana. Nana's lonesome."

She took him firmly by the right hand and led him across the aisle to a seat on the front row while Darwin sucked noisily at his left index finger.

Mitzi watched, embarrassed. What was Mr. Ledgard thinking? What was Mrs. Ledgard thinking? Poor Mitzi, that's what they were thinking. Poor Mitzi is getting a silly old grandmother and two dopey brothers who have bad manners.

As the remaining guests found places to sit down, Frederick's accordion wheezed through

"When I Fall in Love," sputtered around "If Ever I Would Leave You," and whined into "Sunrise, Sunset." Next on the program, Mitzi knew, was the Navaho tune her mother had taught Frederick and after that the poem which Darwin was going to recite.

From across the aisle, Mitzi looked anxiously at Darwin, who was sucking away like a starving baby wolf. Mitzi tried to look happy.

His face red from exhaustion, Frederick ended the haunting Navaho tune, bowed stiffly, and departed. The audience waited.

"Go on, Darwin," Nana Potts was whispering sweetly. "Go on."

"No!" shouted Darwin, removing his Indian headdress and flinging it into a bed of pink geraniums. "He didn't bring his motorcycle!"

Nana Potts became less sweet. "It's your turn, Darwin. They're waiting for you."

The audience would have to wait a long time for Darwin to recite the Indian poem. "Grunch," he said, turning miraculously back into a tyrannosaurus rex, and ducked under a folding chair.

Where was the lady judge? Mitzi wondered. If Mitzi could signal to her to go on with the program, no one would pay any attention to Darwin crouching under the chair. Other folding chairs began to creak as the audience waited. But the lady judge was staying hidden until she got her cue, the last two lines of the Indian poem.

Smiling nervously, Mitzi stood up, walked to the spot where Darwin should be standing, and began:

> From beneath the life-giving sun,
> From beneath the strength-giving rain,
> Here upon Mother Earth,
> We stand in time
> In a moment of peace
> With this man and this woman.
> May their hearts be strengthened,
> May their bodies be strengthened,
> May they walk with beauty before them,
> May they walk with beauty behind them,
> May they walk with beauty above them,
> May they walk with beauty under them,
> May they walk with beauty beside them.

"What an adorable little girl," someone whispered. "So poised. Isn't Walter lucky?"

More important, Mitzi heard the voice of the lady judge. "Friends, we are gathered today to celebrate the marriage of Walter Keppler Potts and Patricia Varley McAllister. . . ."

I did it! thought Mitzi giddily. Her knees turned to pudding, and she sank into her seat on the

front row. Everything around her started to spin, and the ceremony was a blur. At last Mr. Ledgard poked her and said, "Well, they're married now. Don't you want to be the first one to kiss the bride?"

Later, when the guests were sitting at the folding tables to eat the wonderful party food, Mitzi and the Ledgards gave her parents their present.

"How beautiful!" exclaimed Mitzi's mother. "I've never seen a picture and frame that go together so well."

"I was real honored when Mitzi asked me to make a frame for her present for you folks," said Mr. Ledgard. "And I don't mind saying that her picture inspired me to make the spiffiest frame I've ever done."

"That's true," said Mrs. Ledgard. "Horace makes frames all the time, but he's never worked so hard on anything as he did on the one for Mitzi's picture. He knew that picture was special, so he wanted to make the frame special too. I'm right proud of both of them for how it turned out."

"I think I'll hang it in my study, right over my desk," said Mitzi's mother.

"No, you don't," said Walter. "I'm going to hang it where I can see it too. I'll need something to remind me of my new daughter while she's off in the field next month with you and Frederick."

Frederick looked as surprised as Mitzi felt.

"Are we taking Mitzi with us?" Frederick asked. Mitzi couldn't tell if he were complaining or if he sounded pleased.

"It was Walter's idea," said Mitzi's mother.

Mitzi was bursting with excitement, but felt a tiny bit worried too. Was Walter sending Mitzi off with her mother so he wouldn't have to look at her or talk to her?

That worry quickly disappeared. Walter put his arm around Mitzi and kissed her cheek. "I was very proud of the way you stepped right up and recited the poem during the wedding ceremony. I told your mother that you have become a very grown-up and responsible young lady."

"Are we taking Mitzi with us?" Frederick asked again. This time Mitzi was sure he sounded pleased.

"Yes," said Mitzi's mother.

"Wow!" said Frederick.

Mitzi and her whole family shared smiles.

Except Darwin.

"I want to go too!" wailed Darwin.

"Not this year, honey," said Mitzi's mother.

"I WANT TO GO!" howled Darwin.

"I'm afraid you'll have to stay home with Nana and me this time," said Walter. "Maybe Patricia will take you on another field trip sometime."

"NOW!" demanded Darwin.

"Maybe in a few years," said Walter. "After you learn to live up to your potential."

Mitzi's jaw dropped open. Did other grown-ups besides her mother worry about potentials? Then she had an idea.

"Don't worry, Daddy," said Mitzi. "Darwin will learn to live up to his potential. As soon as I get back from the field trip, I'll teach him how."

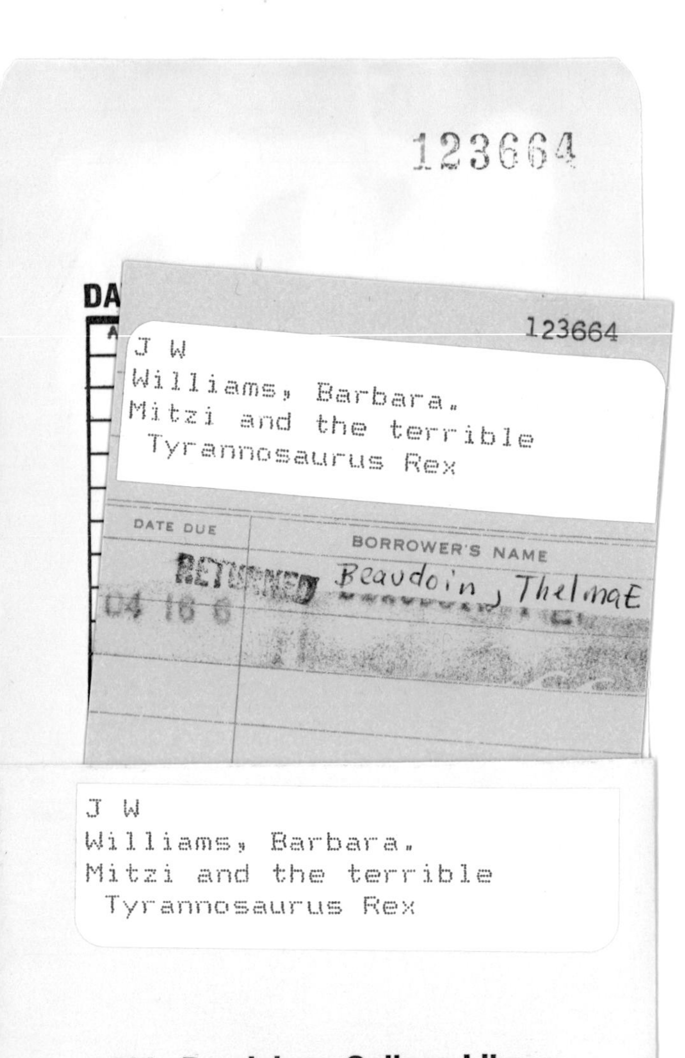
123664
123664
J W
Williams, Barbara.
Mitzi and the terrible
Tyrannosaurus Rex
DATE DUE
BORROWER'S NAME
RETURNED
Beaudoin, Thelma E
J W
Williams, Barbara.
Mitzi and the terrible
Tyrannosaurus Rex